Firedancers

Story by Jan Bourdeau Waboose
Paintings by C.J. Taylor

Stoddart
Kids
TORONTO • NEW YORK

Thanks to my publisher, Kathryn Cole. It was my pleasure.
— J.B.W.

Text copyright © 1999 by Jan Bourdeau Waboose
Illustrations copyright © 1999 by C.J. Taylor

Published in Canada in 1999 by
Stoddart Kids,
a division of Stoddart Publishing Co. Limited
34 Lesmill Road
Toronto, Canada M3B 2T6
Tel (416) 445-3333 FAX (416) 445-5967
E-mail Customer.Service@ccmailgw.genpub.com

Distributed in Canada by
General Distribution Services
30 Lesmill Road
Toronto, Canada M3B 2T6
Tel (416) 445-3333 FAX (416) 445-5967
E-mail Customer.Service@ccmailgw.genpub.com

Published in the United States in 2000 by
Stoddart Kids,
a division of Stoddart Publishing Co. Limited
180 Varick Street, 9th Floor
New York, New York 10014
Toll free 1-800-805-1083
E-mail gdsinc@genpub.com

Distributed in the United States by
General Distribution Services
85 River Rock Drive, Suite 202
Buffalo, New York 14207
Toll free 1-800-805-1083
E-mail gdsinc@genpub.com

Canadian Cataloguing in Publication Data

Waboose, Jan Bourdeau
Firedancers

ISBN 0-7737-3138-5

I. Taylor, C.J. (Carrie J.), 1952–   .   II. Title.

PS8595.A26F57 1999   jC813'.54   C98-931789-7
PZ7.W32Fi 1999

An Ojibway child is unclear about the mysterious purpose
of her grandmother's night visit to Smooth Rock Island.
As she watches and finally joins in the old woman's
ceremonial dance, a powerful link with her ancestors is made.

THE CANADA COUNCIL | LE CONSEIL DES ARTS
FOR THE ARTS | DU CANADA
SINCE 1957 | DEPUIS 1957

*We acknowledge for their financial support of our publishing
program the Canada Council, the Ontario Arts Council, and
the Government of Canada through the Book Publishing
Industry Development Program (BPIDP).*

Printed and bound in Hong Kong, China by
Book Art Inc., Toronto

For my Aunt Martha, the fire jumper,
for Gram who's always young,
and to my family of Firedancers.
— **J.B.W.**

"Slow down, Fast One," Noko shouts after me.
Her soft voice crackles like the autumn leaves
I am stepping on.

   "You move too fast for my old bones," she says.

Though I can barely see Grandmother's face in the dusk,
I know that she is smiling and shaking her finger at me.
I stop so she can catch up, and as I wait, I look up at the orange
and yellow leaves waving from the trees against a fiery sky. The big harvest sun
is sinking quickly, and things that I can see in the light are already beginning
to take on their night shapes. Shadows that were not there a moment ago,
now are all around me. I wish Grandmother would hurry and catch up

I am startled by her long, familiar fingers tapping the back of my shirt, for only Mishoomis used to do that. I jump back in surprise.

"Nothing to be afraid of." She giggles, the sound reminding me of an old loon. Still giggling, she pushes past me carrying her big sack. She shuffles in slow, small steps with her big outdoor boots.

"Noko, let me carry your sack for you," I call after her.

She snorts into the beckoning dark and keeps on going. "I can carry my own sack . . . carried it many times before . . . and still can carry it."

"Here, Noko, here is my flashlight." I shine it on the path in front of her, its beam like a huge firefly pointing the way.

"Don't need a light to see," she mumbles.

Grandmother is walking a little quicker now. I dawdle behind, playing with the flashlight on the trees, making strange shapes. For a moment I think I see something behind the old spruce. I shine my light on it, but there is nothing there.

"Stay close, keep up." Noko warns.

She is too far
in front of me.
I hurry to catch up
and trip over an old
tree root. The earth smells
of pine needles and moss. The shapes around me are growing
darker and bigger. I do not want to be so far behind. I quicken
my step and run to the archway at the end of the forest path.
Grandmother stands, waiting by the old motorboat.

"Start the engine, like I've shown you." Grandmother scrambles into the boat. I start the engine. Its humming mixes with the sound of the waves splashing on rocks.

Grandmother used to ride over to Smooth Rock Island in the birch canoe Grandfather made many moons ago. But Mishoomis is in the spirit world now. Grandmother says she'd rather get to Smooth Rock Island by motor, anyway. I know it's because her arms are too tired to paddle the canoe.

"We'll be there in no time, Noko," I call over the humming of the motor. But she does not hear me. She is hugging her sack and looking straight ahead at the dark island in front of us. I can feel the river's spray lick my cheeks and I smile into the night.

Grandmother and I have been over to the island many times before,
but not at night. And although I am not afraid of the river or the dark,
I am filled with a strange feeling that I cannot explain.

Giant silhouettes against the navy sky look like ancient totems as we approach the shore. The smooth, wet rocks are mirrors in the night, reflecting more shadows. A sudden, circling wind blows harshly in my face and makes my eyes water. It taps my back. I shiver and turn around. There is nothing there. Only the small waves rocking our boat.

"Noko," I whisper, but she does not answer. I see her small form shuffling toward a circle of ghostly white birch trees. They seem to point the way.

"Come . . . follow," Noko motions for me to hurry. I don't need her to motion again. I do not want to be left behind.

We reach a clearing where we are encircled by very old cedars.
Grandmother puts down her sack and moans.

"Ahh, these old aching bones," she mutters. "They need warming up.
Fast One, here's the kindling from my sack. I'll just rest a bit
while you start the fire."

She pulls her old dancing shawl
from her bag and spreads it on a rock.
It is the color of fall leaves in the sun. "There was a time I didn't need
a blanket to sit on." She throws her head back and laughs. It echoes and
hangs in the stillness of the night sky. I watch her long, thin, graying braids,
tied with leather strings, flap around her face like bird wings.
I twirl my own thick braid around my fingers.

I look at Grandmother, and for a moment I see a young girl hugging her knees to her chest. Her face looks to the open sky, to a million glowing fires. I, too, look up.

Then I hear Grandmother speak. "You're a good firemaker, Fast One. Now, come sit close to me and let's watch the flames greet the sky."

We snuggle in silence. Except for the music from the fire, there is not another sound. Just Noko and I breathing.

Again Grandmother speaks, in a whisper this time.
"Your Mishoomis and I came to this island for the ceremonial
dances over many, many moons. And our ancient ancestors came
here before that. Listen for the sound of moccasins dancing to
the rhythm of the splashing waves. Just listen."

I can barely hear her quiet words.

"I will, Noko," I answer, but her head is turned and she is
looking at something in the darkness. I cannot see it.

"What is it, Noko?" She does not answer. Somehow, I feel that we are being watched and Grandmother knows what is there, but she does not tell me.

"I will go and see what it might be." And then I add, "I'll be careful."

Although I try to sound brave, I don't want to go into the dark corner where the fire does not glow. I remind myself that I have been in the woods many times and was never afraid before. I walk toward the huge white pine that hides what could be there. Again, I feel the wind tapping my back. I look behind me. There is nothing.

Suddenly, a loud, throaty sound comes from above the
tree. I look up, and as I do, a large Great Horned Owl circles
very close to me four times, calling down in his eerie voice.
He perches there in the pine, with his big arms open, as if to
reach out to me. His fire-yellow eyes are staring.

I back away. I turn and run to where Noko was sitting,
but she is gone. My heart pounds and my own eyes grow
as big as the owl's. Where is Noko? I want to call her,
but something in the fire stops me from disturbing what is
all around on Smooth Rock Island.

The waves splashing the shore are louder now than they were before. The wind is blowing smoke in my direction. It stings my eyes a little, but the smell is strangely comforting. It reminds me of Grandmother's moccasins, the ones Mishoomis made for her so many years ago. They are old and worn now — just like her, she would say.

Where is Noko? I have to tell her about the owl. Noko will know what message it brings.

Then I see her through the flames. She reaches into the sack and pulls out the moccasins. She fingers the loose beads for a moment before pulling on each shoe. She wraps her old shawl around her shoulders and stares, very still, into the blaze.

"Careful, Noko," I want to call out. The words do not come.

The fire grows larger and brighter. I feel its heat
kissing my face. My eyes are drawn to the intense light.
Crackling and hissing fills the night's silence. I cannot move.
I stand and watch the smoke changing shape, taking on
forms, like ancient warriors spiraling to touch the sky.

Then I hear it. Distant but coming closer.
The beating of the sacred drum, growing louder,
pounding in my ears. And now another sound.
The rhythm of moccasins pounding hard earth.
The wind — or is it — taps at my back

Noko is circling and swirling. Her arms spread, braids flapping, feet flying — just like a young girl. The ancient firedancers from the flames join her. I see reckless, fearless ancestors dancing around the fire. There are thundering sounds and shadows I cannot explain. I, too, am beckoned by dancing silhouettes to join the circle.

"Come! Take my hand, Fast One."

I reach for my Noko's long, familiar fingers. The comforting smell from the fire fills me as Grandmother and I join in the steps of our ancestors. Noko throws back her head and laughs. Her flying braids sweep across my face. I laugh, too. My own braid hits my cheek. We will dance until the night brings the morning star, until the bright colors of the flames turn to gray. Firedancers of Smooth Rock Island. Noko and I.

The huge owl never moves, but I know his message. And I listen for my Mishoomis's moccasined feet.

Author's Note

The Anishinawbe words in the story are:

Noko (Nokoomis), which means Grandmother, and
Mishoomis, which means Grandfather.